Live for You, Kill for You

I0521266

ESUORO

Live for You, Kill for You

ISBN: 978-0-9700599-1-8

CONTENTS

LANE SPLITS & CHICKEN STRIPS

By: Esuoro

EASTSIDE I-20

The passing rush of crisp clean night air muffled the rumble and hum of the engine. Inside the confines of his matte black lid, Jason felt the magnitude of his speed through vibration more than he could hear it.

An obstacle course of double tail-lights crowded the roadway in front of him, as he maneuvered forward. He leaned hard to his left and then to his right, riding the absolute edge of his tires, wearing his chicken-strips down to width of a dime.

"Hey, are you guys there?"

The response was an electronic beep followed by a robotic female voice, "Intercom failed, try again later."

He bent forward, and used his upper body weight to twist his knuckles further back toward his forearm, increasing in speed.

"Keith, Cherie, can you guys hear me?"

Keith's raspy voice thundered across Jason's Bluetooth headset.

"Yeah, we hear you Jay. You need to keep up …we're about three minutes out."

Jason scanned ahead, and saw the single tail-lights of Keith and Cherie weaving their way through the four-wheeled metal cages, almost a quarter mile in front of him.

Jason firmly squeezed his left hand to clutch and then shifted up one gear. He ducked his head and laid forward to minimize his body profile as the side-wind from the sudden burst in speed held the two-wheeled machine perfectly balanced. He felt completely weightless.

After closing the distance between them, Jason joined Cherie and Keith in a side by side formation occupying the three inside lanes of highway I-20 east. Jason rode in the far left HOV lane, Keith in the middle, and Cherie to the right.

"Alright, I'm up. So what's the play?"

Keith nodded toward the dark grey sedan in the lane in front of him.

"Cherie, ease up and take a look."

Cherie eased the throttle and increased her pace forward to the right side of the sedan. She scouted the interior through the side windows, then returned to the formation.

"He's alone, and the prize is in the front passenger seat," she reported.

Keith glanced toward Jason.

"Sounds like the old classic smash and grab. You take the left, I'll take front to slow him down, and Cherie you take the prize."

They continued to follow for another quarter mile, anticipating the blind-spot between the DOT traffic cams.

"OK, go!"

Keith twisted his throttle then weaved around and positioned himself in front of the sedan. Once Keith was in position, Jason reached under his jacket and pulled out a 45, Cherie reached under her jacket and pulled out a mechanic's wrench, and then they both slowly eased forward and rode along both sides of the sedan.

Keith gently began to release the tension of his throttle to reduce their speed.

55 mph, 50 mph, 45 mph, then finally at 40 mph Keith stomped his right foot and squeezed his right hand to hard brake. The driver of the sedan frantically used both feet and engaged his brakes, creating a cloud of white smoke as his tires skidded to a halt. The driver along with all the other vehicles behind them blared their car horns in fury.

"What the ...?" yelled the driver.

As the sedan came to a complete stop, Cherie shattered the front passenger window with the wrench, and grabbed a black attaché case from the front passenger seat. The driver panicked and raised his left hand to guard himself from the flying shards of glass, and with his right hand he reached out toward the passenger seat. He appeared to reach for the case, but instead he grabbed his phone and began to snap pictures of Cherie. Cherie was partially blinded from the repeated flash of the phone. The first flash caught her gazing down at the case as she secured it in her lap. The second flash caught her full facial portrait as she turned her head toward the driver. The final flash was accompanied by a deafening gun shot, and a spray of blood-spatter that landed across the shield of Cherie's helmet.

The blaring sound of car horns immediately ceased. The onlookers from the traffic behind them, attempted to turn their metal cages and escape the scene, only succeeding in further blocking all the eastbound lanes.

"Jay! What the hell…?"

Jason ignored Keith's voice yelling at him across his headset, and he leaned inside the sedan to retrieve the phone from the driver's bloody and motionless right hand. Cherie sat in momentary disbelief, then revved her engine and rocketed down the highway at top speed.

Jason placed the phone in his jacket along with the 45, then revved his engine and took off, with Keith close behind him in pursuit.

The night air was filled with the slow rise of dissipating white smoke and the smell of burnt rubber. All that remained, was the mundane sounds of the passing west bound traffic, a dead man in a dark grey sedan, and the scream of three speed bikes fading into the distance.

THE MAD SCIENTIST THEORY
By: Esuoro

THE APARTMENT

Fatigued, Steve bounced from wall to wall of his small split-level studio apartment. He had to force himself to take a seat in his makeshift home office, a wooden desk with a lamp and two '24 inch' computer monitors. He was four days behind on a major project that was due in two days. But, he couldn't clear the thoughts of Stacy racing through his mind.

He whispered her name, "Stacey Fears."

Steve's fingers hovered over the keyboard, motioning back and forth for a place to start, but his thoughts were completely cluttered. He leaned back into his office chair and closed his eyes in an attempt to gain some form of focus. But the second his eyelids shut, vivid memories of his encounter with Stacy from the previous night, rushed in. He still felt her warm soft skin on his fingertips. He inhaled and smelled her sweet intoxicating scent. He could still hear her sensuous moans and heavy breathing in his left ear. He replayed the visual memory of her firm nipples rubbing up and down across his bare chest.

"Man, Stacey, Stacey ...Stacey," he again whispered, as his cell phone rang.

"Hello," Steve feverously answered.

"Hey, what's up? It's Vill-hellm." Not the call he was expecting.

"I'm losing it," he said to himself.

Steve smiled and laid his head backward against the top of the office chair. He realized how consumed he had become. The term 'fallen' entered his mind. Fallen, over a woman he barely knew.

Vill-hellm was the nickname that Steve had given his best friend William, back in early grammar school. One day, assigned as study partners in presenting a book report on 'The Ugly Duckling', they discovered that the illustrator's name, Vilhelm Pedersen, was the Danish version of the name William. Steve liked the way the name sounded right away, especially the way that he pronounced it, with a long L. He felt that the name had the feel of belonging to a mad scientist, which was an accurate description of their childhood antics, as they experimented in everything. From that day on Steve referred to William as Vill-hellm, pronounced with a long L.

"Vill-hellm, what's up?" Steve heard the sound of traffic in the background.

"I hear a turn-signal ticking, are you on the road?"

"Yeah, I'm in the car." To avoid giving an explanation of where he was going and why, William quickly changed the topic of conversation.

"So, how did things go last night?"
Steve, with his head still resting on the back of the chair,

widened his eyes, and gazed at a single point on the plaster popcorn coated ceiling. He held a strong desire to tell every single detail, but his code as a gentleman, shaky as it was, prevailed.

"Well, I'll explain it like this. You are my best friend, my guy, my bro, and my dog right? The one person, who I can talk to about anything, …well this woman did things to me that I'm not completely comfortable sharing, even with you."

"Oh word? Niiice," said William as Steve continued.

"I find myself in that small space, between the best I've ever had, and feeling somewhat …violated." They shared a moment of laughter.

"So, it was a magic show?" said William.

"Magic? It was like the Cirque du Solei in here last night. She was a very self-confident woman, who was not at all afraid to sexually express herself. Man, I'm still holding on to the possibility that she might call again tonight," said Steve.

"Interesting. It sounds like this one has the potential to turn into something serious. Why don't you make the call?" asked William.

Steve sat up straight in his chair, and rested his left

forearm on the desk, as he reluctantly answered.

"Well there are some complexities involved. She has a son. A little boy, who's old enough to know …well you know. And, she's separated, but in the process of getting a divorce. So I'm playing the situation a little low key."

Steve knew exactly what William's response would be.

"Ooooh, that sounds kinda complicated," they both said as one.

Following the friendly mockery, Steve added, "I know, I know."

William knew that his words were taken lightly, and he wanted to be sure that he had clearly expressed his concern.

"I'm just saying, you need to be extra careful. Sometimes when a woman says it's over, it's not completely over. Especially when there is a kid involved. Hell, we all walk around with a spider web of unresolved ties to people from our past."

Steve listened, but showed no intent to use any extra level of caution. His right arm began to cramp, so Steve enabled his wireless headset and placed his phone on the desk. He seated himself more comfortably in the chair, and was anxious to pass the baton, and hear the details of William's latest sexual conquest. It was his attempt at living vicariously through William, as William strived to live a second childhood.

"Well, enough about my feeble adventures, what's the latest on your mystery lady? What was her name again?"

An unintentional smile grew from the corners of his mouth, as William said the name aloud.

"Cherie, Cherie Waldrop. She called me earlier today. I um, I'm actually on my way to meet her."

William's tone of voice noticeably changed. As Steve listened, the contradiction in William's tone raised surprise. He sounded excited, and at the same time, a bit rattled. His cadence came across as sure and yet unsure. Steve tried to remember, but never once had he ever heard William seem so openly anxious over a woman.

"Oh yeah, she just called you out of the blue? What has it been, about two weeks?" asked Steve.

"Yeah, it's been about two weeks since I last talked to her. Almost two weeks."

Steve easily sensed that there was more, and decided to take the opportunity to pry a little deeper.

THE WHIP

Their conversations had always been a space for open dialogue on any and every topic. But, when it came to emotions and true feelings, their standard rule and shared consensus was the same, 'ain't none of your fuckin' business.' Steve intentionally threw a curve ball, by projecting William's phrase back at him.

"In your own words, sounds like this, has the potential to turn into something serious. I don't know Vill-hellm, if I didn't know better, it sounds like you've fallen."

William quickly replied without thinking, "Nah, nah. I just …we just …she seems like a good girl. She's different."

The words escaped William's mouth with immediate regret.

"Different? So you have fallen," Steve said smugly.

William, now embarrassed, re-positioned himself in the driver's seat as he continued to drive along highway 78 east. The spacious interior of the sedan shrank in on him. He momentarily paused with his mouth hung open, as he consulted the passing highway lane markers for advice. The dilemma: use a defensive denial, or break the rules and give a full emotional confession.

"I wouldn't quite say fallen. Or, even if that was

the case, to use your words, I don't feel comfortable enough to admit that, even to you."

Steve chuckled.

William visualized Steve's gratifying smile of success in exposing his emotions, as the badgering began to pour in from the other end of the call.

"I knew it! I knew it! So, you've been waiting for this one woman, all this time?"

William raised both eyebrows and then engaged the right turn signal and exited the highway at West Park Place. A deep crease grew across his forehead.

"Waiting? It's only been two weeks," said William.

"Yeah but, two weeks for you is equivalent to three females ago. I can't believe this. Wow! I can hear it in your voice. You really have deep feelings for this girl."

William approached the next traffic light, and prepared to make a right turn onto Bermuda road. He became overwhelmed with the unsolicited need to explain.

"It's kinda hard to explain. Since I saw her last, I haven't been able to focus on anything. It's like, I can close my eyes and replay every moment of that last day we spent together. The date itself, wasn't that extravagant. We just had a normal dinner, cruised around town, and saw the sites and city lights. But, it was something about her. The only word that I can think of to describe her, is intriguing. I mean, she was sexy, but it was more than her physical appearance. I mean, she had a pretty face and the perfect body for her size, but it was way more than that. It was like, she had this style about her. In the way that she carried herself. It was the subtle way she moved, the intent in her eyes, the way she focused her smile, and the way she spoke to me, like we were the only two people in the room."

Steve patiently listened as William continued.

"You know how we use to say that, every woman has that one-thing about themselves that makes her beautiful or makes her special? And how, most women don't even know how to use it. Or, they're too busy trying to copy another woman's, one-thing, and end up smothering their own in the process? Well, Cherie was completely in tune with her one-thing. I felt like her one-thing consumed me. It pushed all my buttons and flipped all my switches. If I were to be completely honest with myself, at that exact moment, I was gone. She seemed to be so into me that nothing outside of her seemed to matter. It was just something about her presence. And then, the icing on the cake, was when she decided to stay with me that night. She was so free, she was so open, and she shared all of herself with me. Everything. She was Ecks-quiz-It!"

A brief laugh came across the phone line as William

finished his soliloquy.

Through his own explanation, William had revived the warm sensation and distress within himself. He reached up and pulled down the sun visor, to double check his appearance in the vanity mirror. He deeply examined every detail of his freshly groomed face, as Steve's amused voice interrupted.

"Exquisite? As a man rule, you gotta keep the exquisite girl around. But, let's just pause for a second. OK. I get it. You experienced some sort of feeling, a moment, or whatever, on your end. But what about her? Have you taken into consideration, that, for her, it might have been just a one night thing?"

Steve continued without giving William a chance to answer.

"You experienced this fantastic evening and magical night with her. But then she didn't call you for two whole weeks. And I know that you remember, there's also something else we use to say. The strongest form of love is usually one-sided. That dream come true, that you interpret from a far. But the closer you get, the more reality is revealed. Our mad scientist theory of the moth and the flame. The one game, that if you win, that victory will burn you into ashes. We've always been the flame, why would we ever consider being the moth?"

William closed the sun visor and smirked.

"We? Why did you say we? You know, if I didn't know better, I would think you're really talking about yourself, and your feelings about this girl, Stacey. I mean, a kid and a soon to be ex-husband, that's not even your style. And just for the record, I never said the word love."

William anticipated a sharp retort, as he listened to Steve fumble around on the other end of the call.

Calm and nonchalantly, Steve replied, "I don't know what the hell you're talking about, and I would appreciate it, if you would kindly stay out of my fuckin' business."

The two friends again shared a moment of laughter.

"So, when Cherie called, what did she have to say? Did she come across like she was still into you, the same as that night?" asked Steve.

"Honestly, hearing her voice again kinda threw me off guard, and I didn't really pay any attention to the details. Basically, she said that she missed me, she needed to see me, and then she invited me over. Damn!"

William glanced backward, into an empty backseat.

"What is it?" Steve asked.

"That night, she left her case at my place, and I forgot to bring it with me."

"What, like an overnight bag or something?" questioned Steve.

"Nah, it's a black attaché or some kind of briefcase."

"So what was in it?" asked Steve.

"I don't know man, I didn't rummage through it. It's probably her briefcase for work."

"Shit! If a woman leaves something at my place, by definition it's booty and will be pillaged, pun intended," exclaimed Steve.

William shook his head and smiled, as he turned right onto the street where Cherie resided, Rainbow Boulevard. His anxiety grew more and more, with each mailbox that he passed.

"So, how do you plan to tell her?"

William, confused by Steve's question responded, "Tell her what?"

"Tell her that you are in love with her."

William paused before answering.

"You said that word, I did not say that. But, now that you mention it, I really don't know what to say or ask.

But love, I'm not quite sure if I'm ready for that, not yet. Whatever this is that I'm feeling, I am kinda uncomfortable with it, but I don't think it is love"

"Come on Vill-hellm, listen to yourself, you know what it is. And if you're going to be the guy in love, you have to be 'that guy', all the way. Don't half step. Don't bullshit. Love is not the baby angel with a bow and arrow. Love is a diesel MMA fighter, and if you disrespect him, he will fuck you up. Just tell her. Tell it to her the same way that you explained it to me. Just put it all on the table. That way, you will both know the situation up front. And you'll know, if what you experienced that night is true, or if it's just the moth and the flame."

William took a deep breath and parked his car at the mailbox labeled 4993.

"I don't' know. Maybe I am just the moth," apprehensively said William.

Steve sensed that all William needed was a last minute pep talk. He wanted William to succeed, as he subconsciously felt invested in the outcome.

"Man, you got this. It's first down …and fuck it, you just need to throw the long bomb. Go for it all. Don't hesitate. And whatever the outcome, you'll know that you said your peace, with no regrets. Just make sure, you call me back as soon as you leave. And if I don't hear from you tonight, I'll know, it is what you think it is. Alright? You good?"

William deeply inhaled and exhaled, as he turned the car keys to switch the ignition to the off position.

"Yeah, I'm good."

"Well alright. My man Vill-hellm, going big against the odds. But don't forget …ping me back, and let me know how it went. Good luck man, laterz."

"Alright, laterz," William replied.

WARM RECEPTION

William's anticipation to see 'her' had gotten the better of him. He slowly exited the car, and softly closed the door behind him. He stood beside his sedan, and paused to make one final inspection of his physical appearance. With each step from the car toward the doorway, William's excitement intensified. He stopped at the door and took another deep breath to calm himself.

He made three quick taps on the wooden front door. No one answered, but to William's surprise, the door slowly swung open. William inched inside and announced himself.

"Hello ...Cherie. It's me, William."

William entered and found himself in an immaculately decorated living room. The area was dimly lit by two designer floor lamps that were focused on a large sectional sofa that marked the center of the room. The space looked just as cozy and as welcoming as he imagined it would.

"Cherie. It's William, I think you left the front door open. Hello?"

William examined the details of the room and lost himself in admiring the portraits of Cherie scattered throughout. He smiled uncontrollably, and could not wait to see her in the flesh. He decided to have a seat on the couch and wait. As he bent down to sit, he heard the faint sound of running water. The sound was coming from behind a partially closed door on the left side of the living room. He calmly walked toward the door, softly knocked, and again announced himself. He then gently nudged the door open, but no one was there. He approached the sink, and twisted the handle clockwise to turn off the water.

"Where is she?" he said to himself.

The anticipation was murder.

William left the bathroom and headed back toward the couch, when he thought he heard Cherie's voice. He walked to the rear of the living room, and yelled for her down the back hallway, but there was no response. William checked his watch, and then compared his time with the time displayed on the digital clock that sat on the living room end table.

"Where is she? Am I too early ...her car is in the driveway."

William stepped back toward the front door, and peeked out of the window to confirm that Cherie's car was still in the driveway. The pearl colored SUV was still there, but there was no sign of anyone. Suddenly, an optimistic thought occurred to him.

"OK, she's in the kitchen, probably preparing a romantic type dinner for two."

In route to the kitchen, he paused and picked up a picture frame that contained a full body photograph of Cherie from the wall shelf. As he admired the photo, he flashed back to his last memory of holding Cherie tightly in his arms.

"I cannot wait to see you."

William replaced the picture frame, then quietly and slowly approached the kitchen, as he didn't want to startle Cherie. He turned the cornered hallway and finally there she was, the love of his life. The kitchen was a narrow but open rectangular shaped area, with cupboards and cooking appliances on the left side of the room and a six-chair dining table over looked by two large windows on the right. Cherie sat calmly at the table, staring at the floor. The uncontrollable expansion of William's cheek muscles, produced a smile, with what must have been every tooth in his mouth on display. Cherie did not respond, and appeared to not have noticed William's presence.

"Hi Cherie, I hope you don't mind, but the front door swung open when I knocked, so I let myself in."

As he stepped further into the kitchen and clearly saw her face, he noticed that Cherie was not smiling. She held a concentrated stare at the floor. Something had apparently been spilled. William took another step and noticed that the substance on the floor was a deep brilliant red juice or sauce; that covered the majority of the floor on the left side of the kitchen. Then with one final step, he saw it. There was a man lying face down in the middle of this substance. It was a pool of blood.

BREAD AND BUTTER

An unknown, deep and raspy voice startled William, by calmly inviting him into the kitchen.

"Come on in," the voice said.

After a moment of initial shock, William convinced himself not to panic. The owner of the voice, Keith, stood adjacent to the stove, on William's left. Keith held a gun drawn and aimed at Cherie, sitting at the table on William's right. Briefly distracted, by the size of the hand cannon Keith began to swing in his direction, William weighed his options. Submit and expose his obvious fear, or play the situation from a calm position of strength.

Keith sneered at Cherie, "Is this the guy? Is he the one that has the case?"

Cherie timidly responded, "I don't …I don't know who this guy is."

Cherie slowly raised her head and looked toward William, exposing watery eyes. William interpreted her response as an attempt to protect him from harm. He saw compassion in her tears.

"What is this?" said William.

Keith had already reached his limit, and was even more enraged by William's presence.

"Look, I don't know who in the hell you are, or what game you're trying to play, but what I do know, is that if somebody doesn't produce that case, there are going to be three corpses in the kitchen instead of one."

William again glanced at the floor in disbelief. A dead body was actually lying on the floor in front of him. Cherie was visibly trembling in fear. She began to babble.

"This guy doesn't have it …I mean, he has it, but he doesn't have it on him. It's not my fault, there was nothing that I could do. They wanted money, then they just …they just shot Jay, and took the case."

William was now bewildered and disoriented. He didn't have time to analyze the reasoning behind Cherie's words. He focused only on Keith, the immediate threat. He raised his hands, exposed his empty palms, then he calmly stepped sideways toward the kitchen window. Keith again aimed the pistol in his direction.

"Hold on …hold on," William pleaded.

With his eyes squinted, Keith carefully trained the pistol's sight on William. Just as he positioned his finger comfortably on the trigger, in his peripheral, Keith caught the glimpse of a light in the darkness outside.

"Step back, move away from the window …now!"

After directing William away from the window,

Keith moved in closer trading positions with William. Keith looked out across the darkness of the miniature lawn between dwellings, and he saw that someone appeared to be peeking out of the window next door. William glanced toward Cherie, as she continued to sob and cry. William quickly scanned the room for something, anything to use as a weapon. He spotted a heavy cast iron pan sitting on the top of the stove, and a wooden countertop knife rack behind it. He leaned to his right to go for it, but it was too late.

Keith suddenly ducked down to his knees, below the window sill, and again aimed the pistol toward William.

"What is this? You've got people outside? Who the fuck are you? Where is the case?"

"Hold on. Calm down. Who am I? Me, I am no one. I don't know what this is, and …I don't know anything about a case."

William calmly stepped backwards and to his right, toward the stove as he spoke. He knew that his chance of success was between slim and none, but it was all he had. He was going to go for it.

"Look at her. She looks like she is scared to death. Look at how she's shaking. She would obviously say anything at this point, especially with that huge gun you're waving in her face."

Cherie, still crying, interrupted with an unsteady and cracking voice.

"I came home, and found Jay lying dead on the floor, and the case was gone. Maybe the neighbors took it. I don't know."

Keith immediately turned his attention toward Cherie, with a furrowed brow and a 'WTF' look in his eyes.

"But, you just said that this guy shot Jay and took the case."

William's words began to resonate with Keith. Cherie was afraid for her life, and she would say anything.

Cherie responded, "I don't know who shot him for sure. That 'thing' you're carrying is the only gun that I've seen. I don't know what's happening, and I regret ever getting mixed up in any of this. Just please, don't hurt me! I haven't done anything wrong. It's not my fault!"

Keith returned to his feet, and addressed them both.

"Enough! Enough of this bullshit! If neither of you have the case, then neither of you are of any use to me."

Being careful not to slip in the blood on the floor William continued to ease toward the stove. Just a few more inches, and he would be able to grab the pan and make his move. Suddenly, the anger in Keith's facial expression faded away into an emotionless glare. His focus was solely on William. He carefully aimed the pistol and placed his finger on the trigger. He was going to fire the weapon for sure this time.

Two deafening controlled explosions sounded. William stood frozen, as everything slowed to half speed. He watched as Keith fell lifeless to the kitchen floor. A small stream of blood began to meander across the floor tiles, from a hole in Keith's right temple. William noticed the strong scent of gunpowder had overtaken the room. He looked to his left and saw an image that would forever be frozen into his memory. Cherie aggressively stood with both hands wrapped around a small 25 caliber pistol of her own, with a trail of smoke exiting the barrel.

She was no longer shivering; she was no longer crying; she was no longer afraid. Her eyes were cold and steady, with a slight smirk forming at the corner of her lips.

"Are you OK?" asked Cherie.

William stood frozen, too stunned to respond. Cherie stepped closer with her gun still pointed toward the newly planted body on the floor.

"William! Are you OK?"

William snapped out of his daze and answered, "Yeah, I'm OK."

Cherie grabbed his arm and led him out of the kitchen.

"Good. We have to get you out of here."

As they left the kitchen, William again surveyed Keith's body on the floor, as the blood flow from his head wound connected to the existing pool.

"Who were those guys? I don't understand, what happened here?"

Cherie continued to pull him by the arm, into the living room.

"I will explain later. But right now. You need to go."

Cherie hurried William toward the front door. Still in a state of shock, he paused every few steps.

"What about this mess? You don't need me to help, call the cops or clean this up?"

Cherie smiled with that same soothing and focused smile that William remembered.

"No. I can call 9 1 1, and report a break-in all on my own, but you cannot be here when the police come."

William desperately struggled to understand, how

Cherie transitioned so quickly from crying and shivering to so direct and calculated. And now she stood in front of him, able to wear 'that' smile, as if nothing had happened. Who was she?

"I will come by your place later, and explain everything."

She continued to pull William toward the front door, until he made his final stand. He was shook, but adamant. The clearest thought that William could process was to fulfil the reason that he had come.

"Wait. Wait. I don't understand what happened here, or what you are involved in. But, I came here today to tell you something. I came to tell you …to tell you that I'm in love with you."

Cherie stopped and turned to face William. She tossed her gun toward the sofa, and placed both of her hands on his cheeks. She stood up tall, on her toes, and gave William a brief but sensuous kiss.

"I know. You saved my life."

Cherie then pressed her body against William, and passionately kissed him again. William lost himself in the moment. It was the touch and the kiss that he had dreamed of and longed for. He didn't want to let go.

"Are you sure you're going to be OK?"

Cherie stretched her arms around him, smiled, raised her chin, and stared into his eyes.

"Yes, I'll be fine."

William shook his head, still grasping for understanding, but maintained eye contact.

"Is this about the briefcase you left at my apartment? What's in it, or more importantly, who in the hell are you?"

Cherie just giggled and responded, "In moments like these, you should never stress yourself, over the inconsequential."

She then shuffled William through the door, and out of the house.

THE APARTMENT

Steve pressed 'enter' on his keyboard to launch the last group of reports needed to finish his project. He leaned back in his office chair, and rubbed his eyes with the palms of his hands. The phone rang.

"Hello."

"It's me."

Steve stretched his legs forward and sat upright in his chair.

"Ah, Vill-hellm. What's up? How did it go, did you tell her? Did you throw the long bomb?"

William remained silent for a moment, then responded.

"Yes. I told her. I told her that I am in love with her."

Steve clearly recognized William's rigidness, and speculated that the outcome was bad. Judging by the difference in William's tone, Steve didn't really want to ask, but as a best friend, it was his duty.

"So, how did she respond?"

William again hesitated in a moment of silence, and then answered.

"She kissed me …and I got the very distinct impression that she would kill for me."

Steve grinned in surprise.

"Really? Well shit man, that's a good thing. You win! Vill-hellm one, mad scientist theory, zero."

LOVE AND BLUE LIGHTS

By Esuoro

"Trying, trying trying. That's all I ever hear from you, is trying. Baby …I'm, I'm just tired, too tired. I'm tired of crying, tired of feeling alone, and I'm so tired of hearing you say that you're trying. I'm always, always the one doing everything to keep this relationship together, and I feel like you never put us first. And I'm just so drained right now. I feel like I'm at the point where it's just too much, way too much for me to bear. And I'm sorry baby, because I do love you so much, but I've just had enough. Please don't be upset with…."

Daniel stopped the voicemail recording, and pressed the number one on the keypad of his cell phone, to restart the message from the beginning.

"Trying, trying trying. That's all I ever hear from you, is trying. Baby …I'm, I'm just tired, too tired. I'm tired of crying, tired of feeling alone, and I'm so tired of hearing you say that you're trying. I'm always, always the one doing everything to keep this relationship together, and I feel like you never put us first. And I'm just so drained right now. I feel like I'm at the point where it's just too much, way too much for me to bear. And I'm sorry baby, because I do love you so much, but…"

Daniel again stopped and restarted the message, and continued to listen to it over and over and over again.

The passing cars blared their horns, attempting to let him know that he had parked with his truck still in the roadway, partially blocking the right lane of South Deshong Road. His phone was Bluetooth connected to the truck, so the words from Kim's voicemail played with high definition surround clarity. Combined with the steady repetitious beat of the wiper blades, it all together sounded like a tragic love song. Daniel sat motionless with his left hand cupped around the back of his neck and a blank scowl on his face. A confused sense of failure poured over him. All the stress filled days and nights, working no less than 15 hours, for the bigger house, the cars, the savings accounts, the security, pushing himself to the physical limit to make a better life for his wife, his son, his family. It had all been for nothing. He rolled his tongue on the inside of his lips across the top row of his teeth, and tasted the moment. It was a taste of loneliness and gloom, a fitted match to the weather outside. He slowly began to realize that he had been stripped of his opportunity to succeed at the most important thing in his life; being a father to his son.

As the message started to play for the sixth time, the song was interrupted by the ring of an incoming call.

"Hello."

The voice of a woman in crisis, a frantic voice, echoed throughout the vehicle's interior. Daniel reached for the control knob to reduce the volume.

"Dee, I thought you were on your way. He's still out there, and he won't leave. If you're not coming, I'm just going to call Dekalb County. And ..."

Daniel sharply interrupted. Even though Stacey was the wife of his best friend, he'd never felt comfortable with her addressing him by his nickname. They had never been that close.

"No, no, don't do that! Stacy do not, and I repeat do not call the police. I'm right around the corner and I will be there in 10 ..."

He stopped mid-sentence, realizing that he had unintentionally lost his cool and raised his voice.

He took a deep breath to calm himself, and continued, "...just give me 10 minutes."

The other end of the call momentarily went silent. Stacy responded in a calmer but still somewhat antagonizing tone.

"Well, I'll wait 10 minutes. He just needs to go. I don't understand why Jared just won't leave us alone."

Daniel closed his eyes and thought to himself.

"A man dedicates his life and love to a woman for six years, and she doesn't understand why he has trouble walking away? A man can't just turn that shit off. I suppose I am partial though.''

He then responded to Stacy, "I know, I know. But, I will be there in 10 minutes alright? Just don't do anything and don't call anyone."

Stacy released an aggravated sigh, then said, "OK, 10 minutes."

A loud click echoed across the stereo as she abruptly hung up. Daniel reached up with his right hand and slowly rubbed his face from his forehead to his chin, in an attempt to wipe away the frustration. He glanced at the reflection of his eyes in the rear view mirror. He saw the moisture of tears building. He forcefully pushed his emotions aside, realizing that he had to put his own situation on hold.

He softly said to himself, "My story is not a story about victims, it's a story about hard people, doing hard shit, to maintain and survive."

HAPPY HOME

Daniel arrived at Jared's house within the promised 10 minutes. He exited the truck and approached his boy, his ace, his lifelong friend, tranquilly seated on the top step of the front porch. The slight drizzle had just begun to completely dampen the walkway, but the top of Jared's shirt was drenched. He had obviously been sitting outside for hours. Daniel was a bit frightened at first, as he had not expected to find Jared sitting so calm and peaceful. He sat at peace like a bomb with the timer about to expire. Daniel walked to the steps and sat down next to Jared. He leaned forward with his elbows on his knees, and mirrored Jared's stare toward the street into nothingness. A moment passed and then Jared acknowledged his presence.

"What's going on Dee?"

Daniel responded, "Um, problems. Just another day, in the pages of my crazy life story."

Daniel knew that he was on the clock, so he didn't waste any time.

"I stopped by, to see if you might be able to take a ride with me, and maybe have a little 'vent session'. I need you, to help me clear my head."

Jared turned his head toward Daniel, with his eyes still focused off into the distance.

"I can't right now. I have to wait right here, to see my son. I can't leave, until I see my son."

Jared slightly raised his voice as the anger inside him began to rekindle.

"My wife, no, this strange fucking woman who is supposed to be my wife, she's in my house, and she won't let me talk to my fucking son."

Just hearing the word 'wife' momentarily broke Daniel's train of thought. The word took him immediately back to his own crisis. A reminder of the baron wasteland that was now his life. He tightly closed his eyes and took a deep breath, then reopened them wide, to regain focus.

"Your 'fucking' son? It sounds like you need a vent session, just as much as I do. You should come and take a ride with me, you know, take a minute. We can go, and then come back and see him later."

Jared's slow building rage, turned on a dime, into despair. He responded coldly, as if Daniel was a stranger.

"Nah, I'm going to wait right here. I've made up my mind. She's going to let me talk to my boy."

Daniel started to plea, "Look man, everybody is upset right now, you gotta give things a minute to calm down. She doesn't want to talk, she's saying that she's afraid, and she's talking about calling the police. And you know as well as I, you do not want to be involved in any domestic situations with DeKalb County."

Jared resumed his cold stare toward the street.

"Good. I've sat here for a long time, and thought about it. I guess today is my day to go out. I'm not leaving and I will not allow them to take me. At this point, life insurance money is all I have left to leave for my son anyway. So that's how it will be."

Daniel leaned back, with his arms propped on the porch.

"Man, don't talk like that. We should just go for now, and you can come back and fix things later. Give her a chance to calm down, and give yourself a chance to calm. Then you can come back later, talk things out, and you know the old saying …a break-up is just an opportunity to make-up."

Jared was not persuaded. He shook his head, and rubbed his right thumb in a back and forth motion on his forehead.

"You know what she said to me? You know what she said? She said, that she should have known better than to marry me. She should have known better, because I come from a long line of broken homes and fucked up relationships, and that is all I know, and all I will ever know. She said I can never have a successful relationship or experience true love, no matter how hard I try. She said that I can try and try, but every attempt, will only end in me hurting the people around me."

Jared pushed out a hard breath, to prevent himself from falling into emotional overload, and then went on.

"She said that she is afraid for me to be around my boy, my son, because she doesn't want me to pass my heartless upbringing on to him."

Daniel turned his head leftward in disbelief, and whispered to himself.

"Damn!"

He caught a glimpse of the curtains shuffling in the window behind them. He assumed that it must have been Stacy. Daniel took it as a reminder, and visualized her dialing 9 1 1. The clock had run out. Jared continued his stoned face glare toward the street, as tears streamed down his cheeks. Daniel leaped up from his seat as if to lead in their escape, and headed toward the truck.

"Look man, we definitely need to go for a long ride. Come on, let's go."

Jared broke his stare and looked directly at Daniel for the first time.

With his lips drawn tight, and his words partially shaken, he responded, "But, my son. I can't live without my son."

Daniel continued forward and waved for Jared to join him.

"We will come back, but right now I need you to help me."

Jared, hesitated at the thought of abandoning his post, his line in the sand. The corner he had been forced into and made for himself a place of death's ground. He moved then hesitated, then forced himself to join Daniel in the truck.

VENT SESSION

The masked emotional devastation left no room for idle chatter. The two men rode in total silence, no words, no music, no smiles. Only the silent movie of brief moments in other people's lives, observed from a far as they rode by. Daniel drove to the end of South Deshong Road, and then took a right turn onto Stephenson, headed toward highway 124. Jared pressed the button on the passenger side door to open the window, and then inhaled the fresh moist air.

"So she called you?"

Daniel drove with both hands clinched tightly on the wheel at 11 and 1, squeezing as hard as he could bear.

"Yeah, she called me. She was afraid that you might do something crazy. Hell, I was a little worried myself, when I saw you sitting there all calm like a bomb ready to explode."

Jared snorted.

"Crazy, crazy is the only option that she left me. I have lost everything that ever really meant anything to me. I'm basically fucking lost. I mean, all that foul shit that she said to me …what kind of man must I be, if my woman doesn't believe in me? What kind of man am I, if I can't be a father to my only son? Am I a man at all, if I can't hold my fucking family together?"

Daniel stared into the road ahead, and responded.

"Yeah, you're just fucking useless."

Jared dismissed the attempt at humor.

"This is not funny man. No jokes, I am dead serious. You don't know how this feels Dee. This fucking brawd...? I hate her fucking guts right now, and at the same time, I'm still in love with her. I can't even think straight. And I definitely cannot, and will not live without my son."

Daniel answered, "That attempt to make you laugh, was more for me than you. At least your wife had the balls to say those foul words ...and they were absolutely foul and way out of bounds by the way. She knows how close you are with your family. I imagine, she just said those things to hurt you, the same way that she feels hurt. But out of bounds or not, at least she told you to your face."

Daniel closed his grip even tighter on the wheel, as he saw a green arrow and turned left onto highway 124.

"I wasn't lying to you when I said that I needed a 'vent session'. I haven't told anyone, but two days ago, I came home to an empty house. Most of the furniture ...gone, clothes ...gone, Kim was gone, and my son ...gone. I do know how it feels. But the difference is, you know exactly where your son is right now. I don't know where my boy is, and I have no idea on where to start looking. There was no note, no hint that she was leaving, and no mention of ever seeing her, or my son ever again. And the only communication that I've had with her, was just a cold explanation that she forwarded in a fucking voicemail message on my phone, just this morning. A fucking voicemail message. She blamed me as the reason that she was not happy, and it was my fault for not being there. She loves me so much, but she's leaving. It's like all this came out of nowhere. It's not how I planned it. My story wasn't supposed to go this way. She loves me, but she's leaving."

Jared was finally able to see past his own pain for a moment.

"What the fuck does that even mean? Stacy said the same shit to me. She loves me more than she has ever loved anyone, but right now, she would be better off alone. She said that she needed some solitude to clear her head and that she still loves me, but love is not enough. I thought by definition, if you are in love with someone, it's forever, right? Maybe the word doesn't really mean what I thought it meant. Till death do us part ...bullshit."

Jared physically felt Daniel's sorrow, and was partially consoled that he now knew that Daniel could actually relate to what he was feeling.

"Man, I'm sorry that Kim left ...and that was a cold and selfish way to do it. And I appreciate you coming by to help calm my situation, when you've got your own shit to deal with. But I need you to understand, that I haven't changed my mind. I am going back there, and come hell or blue lights, I will be with my son, even if it means the end of my story."

Daniel listened and realized that Jared was consumed with the prospect of not being able to be with his son. He noticed how Jared was only partially distracted by the news of Kim. He was impressed by Jared's all or nothing dedication, or maybe obsession, as he made another left turn on to Rockbridge Road. He was so impressed, that he began to question his own dedication. Where was his pain, where was his desperation, or was he just better at suppressing those types of feelings than Jared?

"I don't plan on trying to change your mind. My little man is gone. And there is nothing that I can do about it. I don't know if I will ever see him again. I can't be there for him. And hell, in hindsight, I'm starting to wonder, was I really ever there for him at all? I mean, I was working all the fucking time. It was all about work, work, gotta go to work; convinced that I was doing the right thing for him and for Kim. I thought I was doing it all for my family, being the provider. But now, I don't really know for sure. Now that the opportunity to be there is gone for me, it's made me realize the level of how important it is, or in my case was. So I was thinking …you've always been there for your son. You've have actually been there every day. No question. The least that I can do, is to make sure that you don't lose your opportunity too."

Jared raised the passenger side window, as the sky opened up and the random rain drops, burst into a full spring shower. Both Daniel and Jared maintained their focus on the road ahead, watching the street lights illuminate the intersection of Rockbridge Road and North Deshong.

"So you're saying that you are offering to help me get my boy?"

Daniel's voice was direct and unwavering when he responded.

"Yes. If you're little man wants to be with you, he should be with you. We can just go back and get him. But, this talk about hell and blue lights is not smart. Not smart at all. If you're that determined, on being with your son, I think we can find a better way."

An electrical storm of impulses erupted inside Jared's head. He listened for a moment, as two opposing voices debated the pros and cons of the idea and at what cost. Then the voices stopped abruptly. The pros and cons wouldn't matter. Right or wrong wouldn't matter, if his little man could be with him.

"Every part of my being is screaming for me to take you up on your offer, but I can't ask you to do that. And besides, where would I go and how would I take care of my boy, with no real money."

Daniel replied with a crooked grin.

"You mean, where will 'we' go? It doesn't really matter to me; as long as there is a lot of sun, a lot of sand, and a few half naked young ladies walking around. I can't stay here and live an empty life in an empty house. My story is not a story about victims."

The two men continued on their long ride, until the heavy grey evening sky transitioned into a dark rainy night.

THE PLAN

Daniel turned off the headlights, and parked three driveways down from Jared's house. It was their best attempt at being inconspicuous on the brightly lit subdivision street. Jared, sarcastically repeated the plan aloud, unconfident because of its simplicity.

"So, you are going to go into the house, talk with Stacy, and distract her by getting her emotionally keyed up, in a conversation about me, while I walk around to the back of the house and knock on little Jared's window. Then if he wants to come with me, he and I will meet you back here?"

Daniel turned down the interior light, before opening the driver's door.

"Basically, yeah. You don't think it will work?"

Jared scratched the back of his head, and slightly began to feel the gravity of the mission. He recognized that Daniel was now the one with unshaken resolve.

Jared skeptically spoke, attempting to mask his doubts, "Stacy is a crazy brawd …a lot selfish, and a definite drama queen, but she's not stupid."

Daniel opened the door.

"Don't worry. I know exactly what to say to set her off into an emotional rampage."

Then he stepped out of the truck, and left the door slightly ajar. He glanced at Jared through the window and mouthed the words, "Twenty minutes."

Jared tried to excite himself, as he watched Daniel walk down the street toward what was once his happy home. His view of Daniel faded into a silhouette as the rainfall became heavier.

An emptiness grew in Jared's stomach, as he suddenly began to entertain the possibility that his son may not want to come with him. The question, now plagued his thoughts. What if he wanted to stay with his mother? He watched Daniel continue to approach the house, partially pulling his jacket up around his shoulders to cover himself from the rain. Jared averted his attention to the red light of the East Mountain broadcast tower pulsing above the tree line. He remembered how he and Stacy used to sit outside on the porch every night watching that same pulsating light and making plans for their future. Jared closed his eyes and swallowed a huge mouth full of nothing, as Daniel made his way up the steps and knocked on the front door. He looked down at his watch. The time was 8:30 p.m. Jared took a deep breath, and finally accepted the reality of the thing that he was about to do. He thought of his son and questioned himself on what words he would use, and how he would explain. Optimistically, he could picture little Jared walking beside him in the rain. His parental instincts took over, and he remembered that Daniel kept an emergency pack under the back seat. So, he reached over and grabbed the red emergency pack, embroidered with a roadside assistance reflector on top. He unzipped the pack, and found a plastic poncho, under the first-aid kit, flashlight, crank radio, and Daniel's 45 caliber pistol. All the essential emergency items. Jared unfolded the poncho, and reached to open the door, but then paused. Through the faint fog on the front windshield, he saw Daniel's silhouette walking back toward the truck. Daniel opened the driver's side door, shook the rain from his jacket, and climbed in. He shuffled for a moment in the driver's chair then sat still. Jared waited impatiently for an explanation.

"So, what happened, she wouldn't let you in?"

Daniel slowly rubbed his tongue between the backside of his lip and top row of his teeth.

"Nah, she didn't let me in."

Jared then tilted his head forward and pressed his palms against his forehead.

"So, what did she say?"

Daniel leaned his head back against the headrest, looked at the ceiling, and closed his eyes.

"She um, she had company. There was …someone in the house."

Jared froze, stupefied.

"What?"

Daniel straightened himself upright and turned to Jared, hesitant to report the details of what he had seen.

"There was a guy in the house. And from the looks of it, I think I may have interrupted something. She was re-buttoning her blouse when she answered the door and saw it was me."

Jared repositioned himself back in the passenger seat, and glanced out through the front windshield, focusing on the rain drops rolling down the glass.

"There is a dude in my house, getting it on with my wife? With my son in the next room?"

Before Daniel could gauge the effect of this unexpected news, Jared calmly looked him in the eye and said, "I'll be right back."

Jared hastily grabbed Daniel's emergency pack, pulled out the 45, and jumped out of the vehicle.

"Shit!"

Daniel yelled as he scrambled to exit the truck and ran behind Jared to stop him. Jared moved quickly toward the house. He could hear Daniel shouting behind him, but his words were muffled. Jared felt the cool wind and rain soaking his face. He moved in such a daze, he didn't know if he was walking or running. Jared could hear television voices and laughter as he approached the front porch. Enraged, he jumped up the steps onto the porch and crashed the door from its hinges. Daniel was right. Stacy sat on the couch, her face gripped in panic, and next to her, sat some random guy. Daniel entered the doorway behind Jared breathless from the short sprint down the street, and softly approached. He watched Jared's arm muscles flex, from his elbow down to his wrist, with his left hand gripped tightly around the handle of the 45.

The words, "Jared ...wait." exited his lips as a whimper.

Jared heard Daniel's words, but the die had been cast. He thought to himself, that in any other circumstance, he would love this moment. The air completely saturated with tension. Whether in the movies or in real-life, Jared had always loved the sensation and quiet pause, where the potential of violence always seemed to force a person to solidly stop and assess the reality of where they were standing. But, in this moment, as a participant, it was not the same. Jared's cold stare held Stacy and her new friend captive on the couch. From his perspective, it was a frozen moment in time, a first-person view of betrayal, blurred by a mixture of rain and tears.

"So this must be that solitude that you wanted? What's solitude's name?" said Jared.

Stacey opened her mouth, but there were no words. Upon Stacy's non-reply, the guy spoke.

"I'm Steve, and look man, she told me...."

Jared interrupted, "Hello Steve. Nice to meet you."

He then raised the pistol, and aimed it toward the couch.

Emotionless, Jared turned to Daniel and said, "Looks like my story ends in hell and blue lights after all."

The clack of the controlled explosion rang out from the barrel of the gun. Then repeated over, over, and over again.

GOING DOWN?

By Esuoro

THE LIFT

A young twenty-something business consultant, whose physical appearance would distract most men …and most women for that matter, pressed the elevator call button on the fourteenth floor. Cherie entered the empty elevator, relieved that she would have a moment alone. An intermission to the social performance that she routinely pulled off, to maintain her corporate persona. It was hard work being the star. Today had been more stressful than normal, because she had come to work without her personal lifeline. Cherie was both amazed and frightened at how a cell phone had become such an important part of her day to day life. She hoped and prayed that she had left the phone in William's car, as he had driven her to work that morning.

"Vill-hellm, that man is really head over heels in love with me," she muttered.

She pressed the lobby button and then reached down to loosen her rear shoe strap, to take pressure away from her throbbing left ankle. As the doors began to close, a black leather glove attached to the arm of a well-tailored jacket reached into the sliver of space between the doors, triggering the safety contact sensors.

The doors reopened, and there stood a slim, well-dressed young man in a dark suit. Cherie was entranced by his presence. He was completely GQ from his shoes to his collar, with a broad athletic stance. He wore a professionally manicured face, and skin that seemed to have a smooth caramel glow. But his hair, his hair was tightly braided front to back on the left side of his head, with an untamed afro on the right. It looked like a lion's roar. Cherie suddenly realized that she was staring, and quickly turned to her own reflection in the side panel. The young man entered and positioned himself in the empty side of the elevator, to Cherie's right. The elevator doors again began to close, this time with a continuous and very annoying buzz. They stood side by side, with all eyes fixed forward, as the elevator descended. A loud bell sounded from the panel above the doors, to indicate that the elevator had passed the twelfth floor.

With her intermission interrupted, Cherie mentally checked her stage costume, bright eyes with raised eyebrows, friendly smile, and an un-gated stance …check. Her curiosity compelled her to break the silence, so she mentally rehearsed her lines and his expected responses, then spoke.

"You have a very interesting hair-style. It's kind of a rough and rugged contrast to the suit. The combination works well. I like it."

The elevator panel again sounded, to indicate that the elevator had passed the tenth floor. The young man grinned as he turned to reply.

"Yes, I wear it as a sort of deterrent."

Cherie didn't quite understand the reference.

"Deterrent?"

The young man stepped and turned to face Cherie.

"Well one, it is a deterrent to those who would initiate unwanted idle conversation, and I really hate idle chatter. Some people just don't know how to enjoy the silence."

The young man paused, to enjoy the progression of the smile and bright eyed expression on Cherie's face fade into embarrassment.

"And two, it is a deterrent to any who would oppose my will or my desire."

The embarrassment Cherie felt quickly changed into confusion and offense.

"And what I desire in this specific moment, Ms. Waldrop, is my case."

The words stole the air from Cherie's lungs. She flashed back to a memory of a gunshot ringing in her ears, a black case, and a pool of blood on the floor. She realized that her show was over. Her usual bravado was replaced with panic. The elevator panel again sounded, to indicate that the elevator had passed the eighth floor.

The overhead lights began to flutter, then came the thunderous rumble of an explosion. It seemed to be all around them. The elevator swayed back and forth, back and forth, causing both occupants to lose their balance and fall to the floor. The muted sounds of the building fire alarms briefly made their way into the confines of the elevator, and then everything suddenly drew down to complete silence and complete darkness. Only a low fading hum remained. The movement of the elevator ceased. Cherie nervously pushed herself along the floor until she found the corner, then scanned the car for the young man. She saw nothing, hearing only the sounds of movement in the black emptiness, slightly to the right in front of her. The young man grunted as he climbed to his feet, and leaned against the right side of the elevator. He listened as Cherie whimpered in the darkness, somewhere below him.

"Now that was a little bit more than I planned."

The young man removed a lighter and pack of mini-cigars from his jacket. He spun the spark wheel, to ignite the lighter, which illuminated a no smoking sign on his right. He lit one of the cigars, inhaled, and glanced across the flame of the lighter, to see Cherie cowered in the corner. He exhaled. The smoke and stench of the cigar quickly filled the enclosed space. Cherie sat with her legs tightly against her chest and her purse tucked underneath, pulling her dress tightly against her lower body. The last words spoken by the young man, echoed through her mind, my case, my case, my case. She was trapped in an elevator with a man who wanted something she didn't have. She struggled to settle her rattled senses and spoke.

"What is happening?"

The young man again inhaled through the cigar, which briefly pushed back the darkness with a reddish orange glow.

"Well, the interesting thing is Ms. Waldrop, we live in the greatest and strongest country in the world. And whether you know this or not, this great nation that we live in, even though it is the most powerful nation in the world, it has a weakness. And it's nothing new, it is the same weakness that all great nations throughout history have had to deal with in the game of power. That weakness is security."

The young man continued to puff on the cigar as he spoke, briefly providing a light source with each pull. Cherie attentively listened as she watched the reflections of the cigar in the side panels of the elevator. It appeared as if there were four cigars instead of one, but she couldn't tell the difference, from the amount of smoke that filled the air.

"And in our brilliance, we came up with a way to strengthen that weakness, by using distance. By hiding secure facilities all over the nation. But not by hiding behind armed guards or fences with razor wire. We hide them in plain sight. So from the outside it appears as just another store front, just another factory, or just another business office. And there just so happens to be one such business office in this building …your office. So what I've done, is set off a little 'distraction' that some might consider a threat, specifically to that office."

As she continued to listen, she could hear the faint murmur of sirens from the emergency vehicles that she assumed were gathering in the street below.

"And so I've temporarily delayed the emergency power and communications, for roughly five minutes, just enough time for the authorities to make their way up the stairs to address the issue. Once the emergency power kicks back in, you and I, being stuck in this elevator, will have a quiet, uninterrupted, one-way trip down to an empty lobby. At which point, you will, take me to retrieve my case!"

Cherie heard the last sentence echo from panel to panel. In a panic, she thought through her list of defense options: denial, deception, or try to broker a deal. But the young man interrupted her thought process.

"I know that all this may seem a bit much, you know, explosions and everything, just for you. My original plan was to grab you from the street outside or at your house, but I would have needed my partners to deal with the guards outside the building, or your boyfriend at home. But for some strange reason, I haven't been able to get in touch with my partners."

The tingle of electricity moved down her spine. At that moment Cherie knew her current list of defense options were off the table.

"And a funny thing is, two guys that fit the description of my partners were found shot dead, two days ago, at your house."

As the words 'shot dead' left his lips, the young man smashed his elbow against the panel behind him, shattering the reflective material into what looked like a spider web. Cherie just stared at the doors, while her mind scrambled for an idea, any idea, as her eyes began to burn and tear up from the thickening cloud of cigar smoke. She tightly closed her eyelids to prevent her tears from escaping. She tried to remember, if she had anything in her purse to use as a weapon. She had no keys, no nail file, and no cell phone to call for help. Her heels were not even tall or sturdy enough to use as a weapon or cause any real damage. Cherie pondered the possibility of taking him on, in a hand to hand fight. He was a slim guy, and if he wasn't armed, she would have a fair chance to take him with a jab to the throat or thumb in the eye. She first thought that there was no way he got through security with a gun, but then she remembered the explosion. It was too risky, it was possible that he could be armed. The elevator went silent, with only the sounds of the cigar paper and tobacco burning as the young man sucked air through it, along with the whining sound of stressed metal from the elevator brakes below them. Cherie took several deep breaths and tried to will herself back into character.

"It's just a show. Just another show, and you are still the star," she told herself.

The young man heard her mumbling.

"What was that? I didn't quite hear you."

Cherie shed the fear and tension from her arms and legs and pushed herself up the side panel, to a standing position. There was a loud double click of an electronic breaker switching over, and the emergency lights switched on. The lights were slightly dimmed from the haze of cigar smoke. She wiped the corner of her eyes and faced the young man. She examined him in detail and marked a clear view of his neck and eyes, as he continued to smoke. If she could just land one strong blow to disable him she had a chance, but she had to catch him by surprise. The more he spoke, the more her confidence grew. He was not the overwhelming threat that she initially thought. He seemed to be afflicted by a severe form of arrogance.

"If I only had my pistol, I could definitely cure that problem for you," Cherie thought to herself before speaking.

"Do you even know what is in that case? It can't be of any value to you. Whatever you're being paid, maybe we can negotiate a deal between us."

The young man blew a mouth full of smoke in her direction. He used his hand, to cover a coughing laugh as he stood up straight. He was almost impressed at her attempt to stand strong from what he saw as a position of defeat. He looked down at his watch and then back to her smoky silhouette in the corner.

"What's in the case is irrelevant. You made a deal with my employer, and I was tasked with retrieving a case. And it just so happens that I am one of those dedicated employees that sees things through, to the end. But you know what, I'm curious. We have about ninety seconds 'til the lobby. So I'll humor you. How much?"

Cherie froze. She didn't expect him to stand. She would've preferred to attack while he was leaning against the side panel, away from her. So she continued and watched for her opportunity, as the elevator slowly descended.

"Well, I need to know what your price is, before I can make a counter offer."

The young man loosened his tie.

"Now you see Ms. Waldrop, you're smart, but you are making the same strategic mistake that most smart people make in this game."

The floor indicator above the door, flickered and turned on, as its power was restored. Bing, a loud bell sounded to indicate that the car had passed the fifth floor.

"You are trying to politic, when the situation calls for action or what I refer to as 'the hustle'. Now, I know some may think that they are the same but I assure you that they are not."

Bing, fourth floor.

"Politics is about money, resources, alliances, deals, and gaining influence. But 'the hustle', 'the hustle' is about uncontested and absolute intentional action, solely directed toward achieving a desired objective. In other words, I do what I want and I take what I want, and if you can't stop me, shame on you. Do you think that you can stop me Ms. Waldrop?"

Cherie watched steadily in hope the he would be distracted by the bell and look upward to check the panel. She visualized herself, leaping across the elevator and planting the knuckle of her middle finger on his Adam's apple. Her hope faded as she watch the young man retrieve a small caliber pistol from his right jacket pocket. Bing, third floor.

"Contrary to whatever you're thinking, you can't hustle me and you can't stop me. And the fact that my friends are dead, and I know damn well that you were involved, there is no amount of money, no resource, no influence, …nothing you can say or offer me to change what's about to happen to you. You will bring me to that case, and if you attempt to scream for help or cause any distraction what-so-ever, when we reach the lobby, I will not hesitate in unloading every single bullet from this gun into your skull."

Bing, second floor.

They were both taken by surprise when the elevator stopped. The elevator doors opened, and three deafening shots rang out. The young man violently flung backward into the back wall of the elevator, and then fell to the floor. Cigar smoke billowed out of the doors, as Cherie carefully leaned forward, to see who was there. It was William. He stood with a smoking gun aimed toward the lifeless body.

"We have to go, now!"

William grabbed Cherie's arm, and they both hurried to the second floor parking garage exit. The doors closed and the elevator continued to the lobby. Bing, as a result of the gunfire, the elevator doors opened to a lobby full of security guards with automatic rifles aimed inside.

Her veins filled with adrenaline, Cherie blindly followed William to the empty second floor security station, where he had entered. William used his shirt to wipe his fingerprints from the gun, security desk counter and console. He then tossed the weapon back into the weapons cage. They dashed up the stairs one floor, then out of the stairwell across the covered walkway to William's car. He had parked on the third level. William started the car and stealthily joined the line of employee vehicles being evacuated from the parking structure.

After they made it out into the surface street traffic, Cherie felt relieved. She still had trouble understanding the events that had taken place. She stared at William, with mixed feelings of adoration, relief, and perplexity.

"William, how did you know where to find me …how did you get the elevator to stop on the second floor, and how in the hell did you get a gun into the building?"

William turned to face Cherie then smiled and said, "In moments like these, you should never stress yourself, over the inconsequential."

FORCED TO LEAD

By: Esuoro

CLASS TRAGEDY

The sound of child's play filled the room. A little girl, an innocent baby to be more precise, stood silent and emotionless, while the other children scrambled around her. She was, the proper term used today, 'a child with special needs'. Her name was Jadah Black. Though Jadah was a non-verbal child diagnosed with autism, she usually wore a huge beautiful smile, and loved to play with anyone who took the time to show her attention. But today, things were very different. The teacher Daniella Goldman, a special education professional, whom the children called Ms. Dani, checked her watch. It was time for the last lesson of the day.

"Alright kids, it's time to return to your seats. Come on everyone, return to your seats and sit very quietly with your hands on the desk. Look at the sign. Do you remember what this sign means?"

Ms. Dani smiled and continued to wave a huge bright red cardboard triangle above her head, as a visual indication to the children that play time was over.

The majority of the children gathered around her, and all together yelled, "Ms. Dani, Ms. Dani, it means time to sit down."

The children then slowly began to make their way to their seats, all except one.

"Come on Jadah, remember the red triangle means that play time is over."

Jadah just stood quietly, slightly rocking back and forth, as Ms. Dani approached.

"Come on Jadah, it's time to return to your desk, ok."

Ms. Dani was intimately involved with all of her students. She was very aware that periodically Jadah would become detached from the class activities and sometimes would have behavioral episodes as did most of the students. But she sensed something different about her last few outbursts. Ms. Dani calmly reached out for Jadah's arm, to lead her back to her desk, but the instant she felt the teacher's finger tips brush the hairs on her arm, she began to scream. She stomped on the floor, moving in a circular motion, screaming at the top of her lungs.

Ms. Dani responded, as she had been trained, by spreading out her arms to protect Jadah from injuring herself. As she was about to move in closer, Jadah began to remove all of her clothing, and continued to stomp and scream. The other children in the classroom started to respond to Jadah's outburst, so Ms. Dani motioned for her assistant to remove the children from the room. Tears streamed down Jadah's face as she continued to scream and stomp the floor, all of her clothing lying on the ground beside her.

The teacher from the neighboring class entered the room, and found Ms. Dani tightly embracing Jadah. Ms. Dani used all of her professional strength to fight back her own tears. Both teachers cringed at the sight of the dark multi-colored bruises on Jadah's body. They called for the school nurse.

BROKEN HOME

Jadah's mother, Jasmine, was an extremely strong and independent woman. Her mother had raised her that way. She had always been an emotional fortress, a woman who always had everything under control. And now from her perspective she was as a victim, a victim of self-betrayal.

"I am still a stupid little girl. How could I have ever trusted him? What kind of mother am I? I left my baby alone."

Jasmine sat calmly on the sofa, as an electrical storm of self-hatred consumed her thoughts. She stared out of the living room window, with burning eyes, only able to focus on the flashing blue lights atop the two police cars parked out front. The loud and unsympathetic voices of the officers rummaging through her home, to her, was only a murmur in the background. Her older brother Khalil and his wife Veronica walked through the door.

Veronica made a direct line toward the sofa, kneeled, then firmly grabbed Jasmine and held her in a tight embrace. Khalil sat down on the sofa beside his younger sister, not sure what to say or what to do. He held his lips together tightly, and rubbed the palm of his right hand in a circular motion, with the thumb from his left hand. Veronica began to tear up as she spoke through the embrace.

"It's going to be OK. Everything, is going to be OK. Where is the baby now?"

Still in a daze, Jasmine slowly turned her head toward her big brother. When their eyes connected, she completely broke down into an uncontrollable bawl.

"How could somebody do that, to my baby? I just don't understand. Why my baby? My baby loves everyone …why would he hurt my baby!?"

The look in his sister's eyes made Khalil feel completely helpless. He thought to himself, that he should be filled with fire, he should be exerting rage, the least that he could do was to scream at the police, but he only felt weak and inadequate. Jasmine reached out and aggressively grabbed his left arm.

"Where's Kae? You have to talk to Kae! You have to call…"

Jasmine's words became muffled with her sobs, and yet the words still pierced Khalil like a dagger in his side. He had convinced himself, that she knew. She knew that he was completely useless for this situation, and would rather have their younger brother, Kaelan, there to console her. Khalil attempted to fight it, but the self-doubt overwhelmed him. He felt that he was the oldest son, that couldn't protect the family. With the added bonus, he was being a selfish bastard, who could actually have thoughts of himself at a time like this.

"My niece, my little baby niece…"

He couldn't bear himself just sitting there. He rose from Jasmine's side, and walked over to speak with the investigator.

"Excuse me sir. So what do you know at this point?"

The investigator, Detective Bryant, could clearly see that Khalil did not want to be there, and suspiciously asked, "I'm sorry sir, may I ask who you are?"

Khalil calmly answered, "I'm Khalil Black …I'm the brother."

Khalil motioned toward his sister, still openly crying on the sofa. The detective lowered his guard, and attempted to be sympathetic, as he glanced behind Khalil to the sight of Jasmine using her hands to cover her face, and her shoulders uncontrollably bouncing. Detective Bryant opened his note pad and leaned closer to Khalil and softly explained the situation.

"I'm so sorry Mr. Black. And um, I'm not sure to what level you've been briefed, but at this point, from the information that we've been able to gather from the school and the mother, Ms. Black. The party whom you may or may not know as your sister's domestic partner, Terrell Smith, is actively being sought for the physical assault of a female juvenile. Um, the initial medical examination, of the juvenile in question, has revealed that the subject has been the victim of physical abuse on multiple occasions."

The detective paused, took a deep breath, and then continued.

"The examiner also found signs of sexual assault."

The detective lowered his head, as he saw that Khalil flinched and tightened his lips, when he heard the words spoken aloud. He timidly reached out to place a comforting hand on Khalil's shoulder, but pulled back and began to fumble with his notepad.

"We are currently searching the home for any evidence that may help us identify the suspect's current whereabouts. We have patrol cars canvasing the area, and we are checking his last known address and places where he's been seen in the past."

Khalil stared at the floor in front of him and quietly nodded.

"Mr. Black, I know this is extremely hard, but I want to assure you that we will do everything we can to apprehend this guy."

Khalil momentarily remained silent, then responded, "So what happens when you do catch him?"

Detective Bryant looked down to his notepad, and continued to fumble.

"Well, we will take him into custody and he will be formally charged and detained …and at that point, it will become a matter for the court."

Khalil slightly raised his head and looked at the detective from the corner of his eyes. "The court, and then what…?"

The detective held his mouth open, as his eyes searched the room for an answer. He then closed both eyes and took another deep breath.

"I'm going to be completely honest with you. We will probably catch up with this guy, and arrest him. We'll be able to hold him based on the charges being filed by the school and from the mother, your sister. But in most cases like this, the accused usually denies the assault. And depending upon the amount of physical evidence or lack thereof, it then comes down to the adult's word versus the child's."

Detective Bryant leaned closer to Khalil's ear and continued.

"And in this instance, where the child is unable to communicate, it will be that much more difficult to get a conviction. Not to mention the type of trauma that the child and the mother would have to endure during the investigation."

The detective removed the gold plated police badge clipped to his belt.

"Mr. Black, do you see this badge?"

Khalil looked closely at the gold colored detective's badge, nested in a black leather case. The detective paused and looked to his left and then to his right, then placed the badge in his front pants pocket.

"Now, I'm going to say something to you; that I can't say to you, while wearing a badge. And you can interpret it however you wish. I'm not the normal type of detective, who would work this type of case. I usually work homicide cases. I volunteered to come here because …well let's just say I have a really soft spot for children. What I normally advised to families in this type of situation, in the interest of protecting the child …is to handle it within the family."

Khalil again raised his head and stared at the detective. Detective Bryant returned the stare with a stern look in his eyes and slightly nodded.

"Someone in the family, makes things right. You understand?"

He then placed his right hand on Khalil's shoulder, and clipped the golden badge back onto his belt.

"You have a good day sir."

ESTABA MI BARRIO

Khalil struggled to recognize the old neighborhood. Gentrification had erased the surroundings that were once his childhood domain. The area, which had once been a school of survival in the coexistence of the positive and negative aspects of society, was now clean streets, two story condominiums and a community park. As Khalil reminisced in visions of the old days, three short knocks on the passenger side window startled him. Khalil unlocked the door when he recognized that it was his younger brother Kaelan. Kaelan entered the car and shuffled side to side to comfort himself in the passenger seat. He then rested his hands in front of him, and turned toward Khalil.

"So?" Kaelan asked.

Khalil responded with the same as a statement. "So…"

Kaelan exhaled in frustration, and pulled the bill of his baseball cap further down on his forehead. In their history, from childhood their mother had purposely raised them as rivals. And even though they were constantly pitted against one another, the brotherly bond between Kaelan and Khalil had been extremely strong. But, the art of effective communication between the two had always been somewhat challenging.

"So, you've been texting me all day to meet you, and now I'm here. So what's up?"

Khalil reluctantly responded, "You heard about what happen with our niece, right?"

Kaelan leaned full back in the passenger seat.

"Yeah, I heard. Something needs to be done about that, or …I should say, something …will be done about that."

Khalil tightly wrapped his fingers around the steering wheel.

"That's why I wanted to meet. I want to …be a part of that …something, with you."

Kaelan looked away laughing and shook his head. Khalil interpreted Kaelan's laughter as an insult, and went on defense.

"And why is that funny?"

Kaelan, lifted his cap and scratched the top of his forehead, searching for the right words.

"Look Khalil …I know you want to 'do something' with me, but I'm sure that my idea of doing something is far different than yours. I intend to shoot, burn, or otherwise torture the life out of this fuckin' mutt. Whichever option is most convenient. Any grown man, that would hurt a child, deserves one in the head and two in the chest. And I know, that you don't really want to be involved in that type of …something."

Khalil clearly heard the voice inside him unequivocally agree with Kaelan as he continued.

"And there's nothing funny about it. Yeah, I laughed, but please don't take it as me having any doubt in you. I know you've got heart, I know you could handle anything …hell you're my big brother. But we both have our role to play. As bat shit crazy as mom was, she did it right. She pushed you and supported you, to make you responsible, to make you confident and not afraid …the leader. And she gave me complete hell and challenged me at every turn, to make me hard, to make me strong …the protector. Yeah, mom was crazy, but she knew that you would lead us and she knew that I would protect us. So, that is what I plan to do, protect us. I will do my job, and you should continue to do yours. Stay strong, stay responsible, and lead us. The family needs you right now, and I know Jasmine needs you."

Khalil rubbed the palm of his right hand in a circular motion, with the thumb from his left hand.

"That is why I need to do this …something, with you. I am not strong …I'm afraid."

The muscles in Kaelan's face instantly flexed into an expression that clearly conveyed the words he was about to speak.

"What the fuck are you talking about? Afraid of what?"

Khalil leaned back full against the driver's seat.

"Afraid of everything, how people look at me, everyone's expectations, afraid of what people think. I look at everyone around me, and I wonder. I don't know if they feel …safe. I mean, yeah, I can make a decision; I can give some good advice; I'll be there when I say I'm going to be there; I won't let any of us financially fall to the ground. But those small things don't mean anything when it comes down to it. I mean, this situation, look at what happened to our little baby girl. Look at what I let happen."

Kaelan seemed to be relieved and sarcastically smiled.

"Those sound like leadership problems to me. You're taking responsibility. You're having moments of doubt, and second guessing yourself. When it comes down to it, those small things mean everything. They mean everything to us. This situation, is not on you big brother. It's not on you, not me, and not Jasmine. In hindsight, we can all analyze the past on what we could have done, or should have said. How we should have been more protective of Jadah. I'm sure Jasmine is mentally tearing herself to pieces right now. But the truth is, we were all betrayed. As the protector it is my job to deal with betrayal and the things that come after. And please believe, I will do my job! This family business will be taken care of."

Khalil softly replied, "I still need to do this with you."

Kaelan again scratched his forehead, this time completely removing the baseball cap.

"You need to do this for Jadah …or you need to do this for you?"

Khalil momentarily stared at his hands, so Kaelan didn't wait for the response to his question.

"OK. Let's do it. It's going to be really grimy, and if you're going to do this with me, you're going to have to get down and grimy too."

There was silence. Khalil was comfortably uncertain about his decision. He convinced himself that this was just another objective just like any job. It was a goal, with a list of tasks to be completed. He was used to that.

"I guess first we need to find this guy, I was talking with this cop…"

Kaelan abruptly interrupted him.

"We don't fuck with the police, and besides, I already know where he is. My guys have been following him all day. Just meet me back here, later tonight. We'll change cars and clothes, and then we'll head out."

Khalil again responded softly.

"Head out to where?"

Kaelan answered, "Moreland Ave."

The voice inside Khalil contradicted his previous thoughts, like any job this is not.

BACK STREETS

Khalil found himself sitting in the back seat of a rusted and banged up 98 Olds. His inner voice continued to interject self-doubt, and pleaded for him to walk away. Kaelan reached over the seat and handed him a protective mouth piece and a white ski mask.

"What are these for?" Khalil asked.

Kaelan smirked and replied, "For the baby girl."

Kaelan then turned his attention to the sound of the two-way radio beside him on the front passenger seat.

"Alright, I think we're on point. He's leaving 'The Ladie' and taking a left back towards town…," stated the voice on the other end of the radio.

Kaelan pulled his own black ski-mask snuggly down over his face, and then motioned for Khalil to come forward.

"Alright big brother, we're going to switch. You sit in the driver's seat and do exactly as I tell you. No more, no less. You understand?"

Khalil nodded and after a brief second of hesitation, he climbed over the seat to the driver's chair. Kaelan exited the vehicle and re-entered to the back seat.

"Now, I want you to drive slowly up to Lyndale and take a right."

Khalil put the car in drive and proceeded as he was instructed. Kaelan reached under the back seat and pulled out two 9mm semi-automatic pistols. He pulled back the slide on both weapons to ensure that there was a round in each chamber. Khalil glanced over to the front passenger seat as an update came across the two-way radio. Nestled beside the radio, he saw a homemade icepick with its handle wrapped in grey duct tape.

"He's crossing Custer Ave., heading your way…," the radio voice stated.

Kaelan positioned himself on his knees in the back seat, facing the right side back door, as Khalil made the left turn.

"Alright big brother, drive really slow. And when I say punch it, I want you to drive top speed, right out into the intersection."

Khalil tightly gripped the steering wheel, to hide the fact that his hands were shaking. He had just realized the purpose of the protective mouth piece.

"Khalil, do you hear me?"

"Yes, top speed into the intersection."

Khalil then lifted his foot off the gas pedal, to allow the car to creep along at an idle pace.

"Just passed the grocery store, almost up to Beechview…," another update from the radio.

Khalil inserted the mouth piece through the ski mask, and tugged the seatbelt, making it as tight as he could bear. The last update came across the radio.

"Crossed Beechview, and will be there in five …four …three..,"

Kaelan braced himself on the back of the front seats, and yelled, "Punch it, punch it …punch it!"

Khalil stomped the gas pedal, and strained with both arms to maintain the forward direction of the vehicle. White smoke clouded the side street, as the rear tires squealed before gripping the asphalt. They entered the intersection at 55 mph. Khalil caught sight of another car that was entering the intersection from his left. It was a tan 90s model 4-door luxury car. He watched the projection of the 98's headlights slowly grow brighter on the right front side panel as they drew closer. The driver turned his head to the right, just in time to see the front grill of the 98 coming through the passenger side door. The driver was Terrell.

Tires screeched, glass shattered, and the twisting sound of metal filled the air, as the two vehicles collided.

The impact rocked Terrell's car slightly up on its left two wheels and it violently slid diagonally toward the corner of the intersection. Khalil attempted to hold his arms in an extended and locked position, but his efforts didn't prevent him from being thrown forward. He suffered a near knock-out blow from the steering wheel. He could clearly hear everything happening around him, but he could not make his body respond to any of his mental commands.

Kaelan had already sprang from the backseat, and began to unload his weapons into Terrell's car. He moved so quickly that Khalil in his dazed state saw two versions of him. The crack of gunfire filled the intersection, followed by the background jingle of shattered glass and metal thud of bullets entering the car's exterior. Two by standers had approached the accident to help, but after hearing the sound of gunfire, they screamed and ran for cover.

Kaelan walked a circular motion from left to right, with every shot landing in the driver's side of the vehicle. With his vision still blurred, Khalil saw appeared to be a black SUV stop sideways in the street about 30 yards behind the accident ...Kaelan's guys he assumed, but he wasn't sure. Khalil closed his eyes and attempted to shake away the dizziness. The voice inside his head barked commands at him, but the words were coming too fast to understand. When he re-opened his eyes, he saw a blurred version of Terrell crawl out of the back right window and fall to the street. Terrell remained low and leaned against the door to avoid the barrage. His vision partially cleared,

Khalil could see that Terrell's left arm had been wounded, and he held a gun of his own in his right hand. Khalil could only watch. He had an unobstructed line of sight to Terrell, but no gun. He kneed and kicked at the crumpled driver's door, until it partially opened. He then squeezed his way out of the 98. As he fell to the asphalt, he saw Terrell reach over the top of his car and fire one shot. Kaelan fell to the ground …both versions of him.

The barrage of gunfire ended, replaced by shots fired from a single shooter. Kaelan now somewhat dazed himself, crawled away from the gunfire as it grew closer and closer. The men from the SUV ran towards the gunfire with weapons drawn but they were not going to get there in time. A bullet entered the pavement inches away from Kaelan's head. The asphalt debris from the street grazed and broke the skin on Kaelan's face as he continued to crawl for cover. The sounds of the explosions from Terrell's gun were getting further and further apart. Terrell stood with his right arm resting across the roof of his car taking more time to aim. He had a clear shot as Kaelan lay completely exposed. Terrell took a deep breath and stared carefully down the barrel of the gun. Just as he was about the squeeze the trigger he felt a sharp pain in the side of his neck. He turned to find Khalil standing behind him, holding the ice pick with the tip covered in fresh blood.

Before Terrell could process what had happened, Khalil stabbed him in the neck again and again and again. Blood from the stab wounds sprayed into the air like water from a garden hose and then sprinkled to the ground like rain drops. Khalil watched the last bit of life leave Terrell's eyes as he stood covered in blood from head to toe. Terrell's body fell limp against the car and Khalil watched the last beats of his heart as the last pulsating squirts of blood exited the wounds. Khalil stepped backwards away from the body and scanned the scene in a panoramic motion. There was total silence, no more gunfire, no more screaming, and no more voice inside his head. He stood alone center stage as the streetlights beamed down on him. He stood as the personification of revenge, a masked blood stained monster.

His moment of silence ended. Khalil was roughed and wrestled down the street and thrown in the back of the SUV. The tires of the SUV squealed, as they escaped the scene. Khalil sat calmly in a place of blood soaked peace. He looked to his right and stared as his little brother held his left shoulder in agony. Kaelan stared back and shared a painful smile.

"You saved my life. And the family business is settled. I guess this time you are the leader …and the protector."

Khalil thought back to his brother's words from earlier in the day. Kaelan was right. He didn't want to be involved in this. He hadn't wanted this at all. He removed the bloody ski-mask and pressed his top and bottom lips firmly together, in an attempt to hide his remorse. Khalil realized that he had not only taken a life and left a body in the street, he had left a piece of himself there as well.

He felt the rewards of what he now saw as a selfish quest. A quest to validate a position that he already held.

"Yeah, I guess sometimes we get exactly what we ask for."

MEASURED BY THE
NUMBERS
By: Esuoro

THE SQUADROOM

Detective David Bryant started to feel the distinct sensation that he could not breathe.

"David, I just called to tell you that I'm sorry for my part in what happened when you left this morning. I really hate it when we argue in the mornings. For me, it ruins the whole day. I usually find myself, searching for a place to hide and cry before lunch."

The detective squeezed his cell phone in fury, wishing that he had the hand strength to crush and shatter the device into a million pieces.

"It's alright, I hate when we argue in the mornings too."

Carla was relieved. "Well, I guess I'll let you get back to work. I have to get Samantha ready for the school bus. Do you want to speak to her, and wish her a good day at school?"

The detective pressed his lips together tightly, as his heart skipped a beat and a surge of emotion began to push its way up from his abdomen through his chest.

"Umm no, you can tell her for me."

His wife paused and wanted to question the response. She thought to herself, could he really be so upset, that he did not want to speak to his daughter? She didn't want to sour the freshly made peace treaty and apology, so she decided to say nothing.

She simply replied, "Well OK, you have a good day OK baby. Oh, and by the way …you left without your badge this morning."

"Alright. I will get it when I get home this afternoon. I will probably be in the office all day, so I won't need it."

"Ok, I will leave it on the night stand for you."

"Alright. Talk to you later."

Frustrated, he didn't wait for a good-bye, and hung up.

"I am in a never ending hell."

The detective reached back to throw his cell phone across the room, to enjoy the release and pleasure of watching it violently crash into the wall, until he was suddenly distracted.

"What is this girl doing? She knows that she can't bend over her desk like …ooh man."

Detective David Bryant sat down at his desk, then picked up his empty coffee mug and held it to his lips, to conceal the jaw-drop expression on his face. He focused across the top rim of the mug, as Officer Brown leaned seductively across her desk for a stapler, pencil sharpener, or whatever. He glanced up and then down the split rows of desks, to make sure that he wasn't being observed while he was observing the visual dessert in front of him. There were very few women that could make the official blues look even half way decent. But, even the gaudy police uniform couldn't hide the appealing invitation from her perfectly sized breasts, and her thick juicy thighs, leading up to her perfectly shaped apple bottom. Brown arched her back muscles in the tightly fit top, as she leaned over further and further. The visual stimulation was just too much.

"Why are opportunities to fuck up, so plentiful?" the detective murmured.

"What did you say?"

"Oh, nothing."

The detective placed the coffee mug on his desk, bent forward in his chair and held his head down. He attempted to use his left hand to wipe the image from his eyes but no such luck.

"Don't you just hate 10-16s? I absolutely loathe them. We had the worst 10-16 call last night. When my partner and I arrived on scene there was a young couple at each other's throats. They were screaming, cursing and throwing shit at each other. It was just a complete spectacle in their own front yard no less. So, we finally got them separated, right? My partner cuffed the husband while I tried to use my womanly solidarity to get the wife to open up to me. I told her the usual …you know, if he had put his hands on her or even if she felt threatened that we would take him away. I could tell that she was hurt and in pain even though she didn't have any visible bruises. And I guess to be fair, the husband looked a little banged up as well. I mean they were really going at it. I explained to her that she didn't have to be afraid and that if she wanted help all that she had to do was to tell me. And do you know what this ratchet princess said to me?"

Brown returned to her chair, rolled backwards toward the detective's desk, and turned to face him. Detective Bryant shrugged his shoulders, and removed his hand from his eyes. Brown continued her story and added animation to mimic the subject. The detective involuntarily focused on her tightly fit top and her voluptuous breasts as they danced up and down back and forth with her movement.

"This woman said, and I quote, 'I don't have anything to say to you and I don't need or want your help. We don't fuck with the police.' I was completely stunned, you know. Her response caught me off-guard for a moment. So, I asked her, why? She looked at me with this confused and frustrated expression on her face and said, and again I quote, 'Because y'all kill young black men for sport and I don't want you to kill my husband.' I motioned to my partner to remove the cuffs. We just got back in the squad car and left, you know. I don't mean to be heartless because as a black woman I can completely understand her point of view. But at the same time …her husband could beat her ass up and down the street with a baseball bat on video and I would never go back there to help her. She pretty much called me a murderer. Do you believe that? I absolutely hate 10-16s."

Detective Bryant pushed out a fabricated sound which he had hoped would be interpreted as an amused grunt. An attempt to disguise the war of stimulation versus depression which was at the height of battle inside him. He again allowed himself to bask in the full alluring glow of the young beautiful woman that sat before him almost half his age. The detective caught himself, then again slumped downward into his chair. His body language matched his internal feelings, a conflicted and defeated man. He pulled a cigarette from his left jacket pocket, lit it, and took a deep stress-relieving pull.

A thunderous voice shattered the silence.

"Who in the hell is smoking in my squad room?"

Captain Gerald Flint entered from the hallway, and stormed through the room toward his office at the far end of the rows of desks.

"Bryant is that you? What the hell is wrong with you? You can't smoke in here!"

Detective Bryant extinguished the cigarette in his empty coffee mug and stood.

"We need to talk! In my office, now," yelled the captain.

As the detective rounded his desk, Brown grabbed his arm and said, "Wait."

She paused, looked up at him eye to eye and continued, "Are you OK?"

The detective immediately froze. Even though he could not actually feel her physical touch through the fabric of his sport jacket, a tingling sensation of icicles started slowly spinning around his arm.

"Honestly …I don't know."

Officer Brown reluctantly smiled, nodded and then gingerly released her grip on detective Bryant's arm.

THE FINE LINE

Captain Flint was a tough old bastard. He had worked homicide in DeKalb County for decades. He was the stereo-typical, hard as nails, mean as hell police captain straight off of a 1990s action movie set. That quality was the main reason that Detective Bryant held the highest respect for him. The captain stood behind his desk holding a group of case folders in his crossed arms. He went completely ballistic, even before Detective Bryant could get both feet passed the office door.

"What the hell is going on with you Bryant? You used to be hot shit, the top dog homicide PO-LICE. You used to be able to clear the toughest cases in days. With you, there was no such thing as unsolvable. You were cocky as hell and I used to hate your fuckin' guts, but you were good. Now, I look at you and you're falling off son …way off. I got murders building up. Just look at that board out there. All I see is red, red, red and more red. It looks like a giant maxi-pad on the wall and it's not even my time of the month. And the logs show that you've been sitting slow and cold on the same four cases for the past three weeks. Unfortunately son, we are in a profession where our performance is measured by metrics, by the numbers. And right now your numbers are a big pile of dog shit. I know the last few months have been a tough time for you but you need to tell me right now, can you still handle it?"

Captain Flint uncrossed his arms and slammed the case folders on his desk.

"Look at this shit. Case# 1, a double homicide: 4993 Rainbow Blvd., two adult males found shot dead in the kitchen of a private residence. Case# 2, another double homicide: adult male Steve Shaw and adult female Stacey Fears found shot dead in private residence, husband and male juvenile missing. Case# 3: unknown adult male found in elevator, shot dead, office building downtown Decatur."

The captain clearly saw the shameful expression that began to form on Detective Bryant's face, he pressed on.

"Oh, I can go on, Case# 4: person of interest, one Terrell Smith, found dead…"

The detective sharply interrupted.

"I'm only working two open cases. That first double, 4993 Rainbow, that case was closed as a self-defense case during a home invasion. The weapon recovered from that case was tied to the I-20 homicide a few weeks back. The Shaw and Fears double is open and we have a statewide Amber alert out for the husband and missing juvenile, but no leads. And the Feds are all over the elevator guy, I haven't been able to get anywhere near that one. They mentioned something about a missing briefcase, then they shut me out. They aren't sharing any information at all."

The detective looked downward, partially filled with guilt and ran his thumb across the section of his belt where he normally wore his badge.

"As far as the last case, person of interest Smith …that was …um, that was a 'flee from the scene' of a traffic collision. So, I pushed that one back over to Traffic."

Captain Flint shook his head and calmly walked around the desk to close his office door.

"You pushed it back to Traffic? The subject had four pencil sized holes in his neck, gun casings and bullet holes were everywhere, and a bloody icepick was found not three feet away. And you really think that was from a traffic collision? Come on man."

Detective Bryant knew that his creative report on the Smith case wouldn't go very far if scrutinized. He had hoped that the omitted details would go unnoticed. No one was usually concerned about the death of a person of interest on the run, especially a person of interest in a child molestation case. Bryant had made peace with his actions. He felt that if he was wrong, so what. Another monster who hurt children was off the streets. He was prepared to pay the consequence.

The two men were interrupted by a muffled ringing noise. The detective fumbled through his jacket pocket to retrieve his cell phone. The display read 'Carla'. He quickly pressed ignore and disabled the ringer volume. The captain scratched the balding spot on the top center of his head and proceeded back to his desk chair and sat. He motioned for the detective to take a seat and just stared at Bryant. He knew something smelled wrong, but decided he did not want to know.

"Look Bryant, I know you've got a lot going on, but I want you to know, that I care, and at the same time, due to recent events, I don't care. I know that makes me a cold son of a bitch, but what else is new? You can't lose your shit on me right now. I need you. Falling apart, that's not an option for you right now. I need you to put all of your personal issues on hold. The shit is literally hitting the fan and I really need you. The top-dog homicide version of you. Now listen."

Captain Flint pulled a sealed case file from his briefcase.

"I just attended an executive brief on a homicide that occurred around 4AM this morning in Avondale. The initial reports show that the state of the victim in this particular homicide matches the M.O. of victims in seven other homicide cases in the metro area. Four in Fulton County, being worked by Atlanta PD and three from Henry County."

Detective Bryant was intrigued, and leaned to the edge of the seat.

"A serial, in Atlanta?"

"Yes, that's what the Feds believe at this point. They are planning to form a task force with the six main metro area counties', but for right now, I need you to take point on the Avondale case."

Detective Bryant's left leg began to bounce repeatedly and he felt the vroom-vroom of his mind beginning to race. The captain was somewhat relieved to see the fire re-ignite in the detective's eyes. With an unwilling half smile he pushed the file across his desk and continued.

"The four …oh I'm sorry, the two cases that you were working will go back on the board and you will work this case, exclusively. Until the task force members are assigned officially, all information will flow through me and me only. This is not public knowledge. It's for executive brass only and it needs to remain that way. Since you and Officer Brown seem to get along so well, I want you to partner with her on this one. You've done a pretty good job mentoring her thus far and she's earned her shot to play in the big game. A trial by fire."

Detective Bryant now fully attentive, eagerly picked up the file and stood to leave the captain's office.

"Bryant, don't fuck this up. You can handle this, right? I told the Feds that I would assign my best resource. You do know what that means?"

Detective Bryant smiled and replied, "Yes Sir, it means that I'm going to catch a serial killer."

Captain Flint shook his head.

"Now, there's the cocky bastard that I used to know."

BUCKETS OF BLOOD

The rear tires of Detective Bryant's black SUV screeched as he made a sharp left onto Sam's Crossing from East College Avenue. Buzzing from the adrenaline pulsating throughout his system, he weaved in and out of traffic. After visiting the Avondale crime scene his mind was once again consumed with analytical thoughts. What seemed like meaningless details, scenarios and possibilities were all waiting for him to put them in their proper place. They were begging for him to put them in their destined order, the order that would pave the way to finding the person responsible. Detective Bryant was not only thinking like his old self, he felt like his old self and he loved it. He had clear thoughts, and he could breathe again, a completely focused mind. Officer Brown was nervous and excited to be part of the team, now that they were on special assignment. She had changed from the uniform blues into even sexier casual street attire. She sat quietly dazed in the passenger seat, while Detective Bryant fought the distraction of her extremely intoxicating scent. On cue, as if his wife Carla could read his mind, Bryant's cell phone began to vibrate in his jacket pocket.

"Somebody is really trying to get a hold of you. Your phone has been buzzing all morning."

Detective Bryant continued to focus on the road ahead.

"It's just my wife. I'll call her back later."

Officer Brown responded with a practiced smile, but her thoughts were still consumed with a vision of horror she couldn't shake.

"Bryant, did you know that I worked in traffic for my first six months. After all the collisions and mangled bodies that I have seen, I thought I had a clear definition of the word gruesome, but what we just saw, it doesn't compare at all. That crime scene was a fucking nightmare," said Brown.

Bryant was still partially engaged in mentally examining the images and he responded calmly, "Yeah, I was just thinking the same thing. Two metal buckets of blood and body parts thrown everywhere. There has to be some sort of significance behind the two metal buckets. Those old buckets are not as common as they used to be."

Brown's attempt to hide how disturbed she felt from what she saw at the scene became more evident with each question.

"The thing that I don't understand is, how could someone take the time to completely drain a body and cut it up into that many pieces without a witness seeing or hearing anything? I mean, if the killer committed the act onsite or even dumped the body parts there later, that would take a lot of time, right?"

"Yeah I agree, that's a good question; a drained body and not one drop of blood on the ground. First, we need to establish a window from when the last time someone was in the area to when the remains were found."

Still rattled Brown exhaled a deep breath and said the words again in disbelief, "Buckets of blood. Wow, I would have never guessed, that I would ever use that term in the literal sense. So, where are we off to in such a hurry?"

"Well, I want to contact our counterparts at Atlanta P.D. and examine the four scenes in Fulton. We should be able to establish a window of time for each scene, and check the victim profiles for any similarities. Ah Shit! I'm going to need my badge, damn."

The detective flipped on his blue lights, then breached the curb on both sides of Ponce de Leon Avenue to complete a U-turn. He was headed for home.

HOME SWEET HOME

As the Detective Bryant turned into his driveway, he was surprised to see that Carla's car still sat parked in the same place as when he left for work.

"Fuck me."

Officer Brown looked up and scanned the house, yard and neighboring homes. Everything seemed to be normal. It was just an average eastside suburban neighborhood. She squinted, confused by his sharp change in demeanor.

"Something wrong?"

"My wife is home."

He suddenly lost focus and began to feel short of breath.

Brown asked jokingly, "Should I just wait in the truck? I don't want to be involved in a 10-16."

The detective took a second to gather his thoughts.

"Um, yeah that may be best."

He closed his eyes and took a long deep breath then opened the driver's side door.

"On second thought, here, take the keys. If I'm not back in 15 minutes, just drive down to the Shoppe and order lunch for us. This may take a while, but I should be ready by the time you get back."

"You actually want to eat lunch, after that crime scene?" asked Brown.

Detective Bryant exited the vehicle and closed the door.

"You get used to it."

Bryant slowly approached his front door. He closed his eyes and prayed.

"Please let her be asleep, I can't deal with this right now. Please, please, please."

He unlocked the door and entered as quietly as possible. As he headed toward the back bedroom, he heard his name being called from the kitchen.

"David? Hey honey, I guess you needed your badge after all."

Carla met him in the hallway, wearing a faded blue robe and bedroom slippers. She gave him a huge hug and kissed him on his cheek. Detective Bryant reluctantly returned her embrace and kiss.

"Hey, what are you doing home, is everything ok?"

Carla felt relieved and happy to see him. She smiled and gazed deeply into his eyes.

"Yes, everything is fine. Samantha didn't feel well this morning, so I decided to keep her home from school."

Detective Bryant immediately released his embrace and turned away. He started to inch his way toward the bedroom.

"Oh um, well, I just stopped by to get my badge. The captain has assigned me to an important case."

Carla followed and reached for his arm, but Bryant moved forward just out of her reach.

"Aww, I was hoping that you could stay with us for a little while. I feel like I never get to spend time with you, and you know your daughter misses you. We tried to call you earlier; Samantha left you a really cute message. Did you hear it?"

Detective Bryant firmly bit his bottom lip.

"I wish I could stay baby, but my new partner is waiting outside."

He continued toward the bedroom.

"You have a new partner?"

Bryant entered the bedroom and retrieved his badge from the nightstand.

"Yeah, you remember the young lady that I have been mentoring, Officer Brown. I think that I've mentioned her to you before. Well she has been promoted to work with me on this case, on a trial basis."

Carla stood in the middle of the hallway as Bryant attempted to leave. Her smile slowly transitioned into disappointment as she realized that he was indeed about to walk out the door.

"Oh, well …you seem excited. This must be a really important case."

Detective Bryant stepped closer, placed his hands on her shoulders and kissed her forehead.

"It is, it's a huge case for the department. Maybe even bigger."

Carla folded her arms across her chest and continued to hold her post in the middle of the hallway. She did not share in his excitement.

"Are you at least going to check on your daughter, before you rush off to work?"

Detective Bryant removed his hands and placed them at his side. He stood and stared into Carla's eyes for the first time since he had arrived.

"She's been asking for you all day. You can't take a few minutes to check on her, and remind her that you love her?"

Detective Bryant leaned to his right, then turned and put his back against the wall. Carla firmly grabbed his arm and almost forcefully pulled him toward their daughter's room.

"She understands that you have to work, but she misses you and so do I."

Carla entered the room, then walked over to the edge of the bed and sat. Bryant remained in the doorway.

"Hey, I didn't mean to wake you. Are you feeling any better? Look who's here, its daddy. Daddy came home, all the way from work, just to check on you, his little angel."

Bryant leaned against the door jamb and stared at the floor in front of him. Carla glanced toward her husband and motioned for him to join her at the bedside. Detective Bryant remained still. Carla smiled, as if to make an excuse for his behavior and she furiously darted across the room.

"David, what is wrong with you?" Carla softly yelled, attempting to not upset their daughter.

"That's your daughter. Is your job or this case really that important to you? So important, that you would put it before your family!"

Bryant continued to stare at the floor.

"Carla, you cannot say that to me."

"Well, what is going on? Why won't you even look at her? Look at her! Look at your daughter!"

Detective Bryant felt the surge of emotion again begin to stir and push upward. He closed his eyes and tried to contain it, but it violently forced its way through. Bryant grabbed Carla by the arms and forced her backward against the bedroom door. He didn't exert much force, but the door gave way and thumped loudly against the hollow bedroom wall. The sound stunned Carla.

"No! No! I can't do this anymore. You look! You look at that bed and tell me what you see."

Carla's initial fury was replaced with panic. All the anger and all the frustration that Bryant had long kept buried was now on the surface. The intensity in his eyes kept her frozen as the corners of her eyes, now widely open, began to fill with tears of fear.

Bryant released her right arm and banged his left fist against the door.

"Tell me what you see!"

Carla was too afraid to turn her head or even move at all. A steady stream of tears began to pour down Bryant's cheek, but his facial expression remained hard and cold.

There is no one in the bed Carla. Samantha is not here. Our baby girl is gone."

Carla's pupils moved back and forth, focusing on Bryant's left eye, then his right eye, and then back again. Bryant's voice cracked from distress, as he repeated himself.

"Our little, sweet, innocent baby girl is gone. You have to stop this Carla. It's time to stop."

Carla forcefully shut her eyes and began to fall to her knees. Bryant repositioned his arms, and tried to hold her up and support her weight against the door.

"No baby, no. I need you to open your eyes and look at that bed. Tell me what you see."

She refused and shook her head from side to side, her eyes tightly shut.

"Carla, now come on baby, just look. Look and tell me what you see."

Carla opened her eyes reluctantly. Her eyelids were heavy, her lashes soaked with tears. Her vision was blurred but she could see clearly that her husband was fighting to hold back emotions of his own.

"I need you to do this, do it for me."

Carla softly placed her hands on Bryant's chest, and slowly she peered over his shoulder. Their daughter's bed was empty. Bryant attempted to catch her, as she cried out, fell limp and slid down the bedroom door, inconsolable. They sat and held each other on the floor, and again relived the pain of mourning the loss of their daughter Samantha.

After he regained his composure, finally Bryant was able to bring Carla to her feet and get her to bed.

"Here baby, take your medicine and have a drink of water."

He sat with Carla and rubbed his hand repeatedly across her neck and upper back until she was completely calm. She had just fallen asleep, when Bryant heard his truck pull up out front.

He gently kissed Carla's forehead and whispered, "We're going to be OK baby. I'll be back soon."

Detective Bryant got up quietly and headed toward the front door. He stopped at the hallway bathroom, and turned on the light to make sure that there was no remaining evidence of tears around his eyes or on his face. He made eye contact with himself in the mirror and took a long deep breath. He stared at himself, only partially recognizing his reflection.

"I am in a never ending hell. A hell of my own choosing. How much longer can I deal with this? How long will it be before this happens again? How many times are too many? I love her, so is there such a number? What am I going to do next time? Next time."

He reached over to the switch and turned off the light.